Farm Animals

Cattle

Sharon Dalgleish

CHELSEA CLUBHOUSE

An Imprint of Chelsea House Publishers
A Haights Cross Communications Company
Philadelphia

Chelsea House Publishers
2080 Cabot Boulevard West, Suite 201
Langhorne, PA 19047-1813

The Chelsea House world wide web address is www.chelseahouse.com

First published in 2005 by
MACMILLAN EDUCATION AUSTRALIA PTY LTD
627 Chapel Street, South Yarra, Australia, 3141

Associated companies and representatives throughout the world.

Visit our website at www.macmillan.com.au

Library of Congress Cataloging-in-Publication Data

Dalgleish, Sharon.
    Cattle / Sharon Dalgleish.
    p. cm. -- (Farm animals)
    Includes index.
    ISBN 0-7910-8270-9
    1. Cattle--Juvenile literature. I. Title.
    SF197.5.D35 2005
    636.2--dc22

                                                            2004016188

Edited by Ruth Jelley
Text and cover design by Christine Deering
Page layout by Domenic Lauricella
Photo research by Legend Images
Illustration by Luke Jurevicius

Printed in China

Acknowledgments

The author and the publisher are grateful to the following for permission to reproduce copyright material:

Cover photograph: cows in a field, courtesy of Stockbyte.

Australian Picture Library, p. 22; Australian Picture Library/Corbis, p. 29; BrandX Pictures, pp. 18 (bottom), 30; The DW Stock Picture Library, pp. 8 (center), 10; Getty Images/Photodisc, pp. 5, 12, 24, 27; ImageAddict, p. 13 (center and bottom); Image Library, p. 13 (top); Jiri Lochman/Lochman Transparencies, p. 28; © Peter E. Smith, Natural Sciences Image Library, p. 8 (bottom right); Photodisc, pp. 3, 15, 18 (top), 19 (top and bottom), 21 (top); Photolibrary.com, pp. 7, 8 (top), 9, 11, 20 (top), 25; Photolibrary.com/Animals Animals, p. 16; Photolibrary.com/Super Stock, p. 26; David Hancock/Skyscans, p. 17; Stockbyte, pp. 1, 4, 14, 20 (bottom); United States Department of Agriculture, pp. 6, 8 (bottom left), 21 (bottom), 23.

While every care has been taken to trace and acknowledge copyright, the publisher tenders their apologies for any accidental infringement where copyright has proved untraceable. Where the attempt has been unsuccessful, the publisher welcomes information that would redress the situation.

Contents

What Are Cattle?

Cattle is the word for cows and bulls. Cattle are big, strong animals. Most are a shade of brown, black, or white. They all make a deep "moo" sound.

Cattle can have large spots or stripes.

The adult female is called a cow. The adult male is called a bull. The young are called calves. A group of cattle is called a herd.

Cattle mostly live in herds.

Cows

Cows give birth to calves. The calf drinks milk from the cow's **udder**.

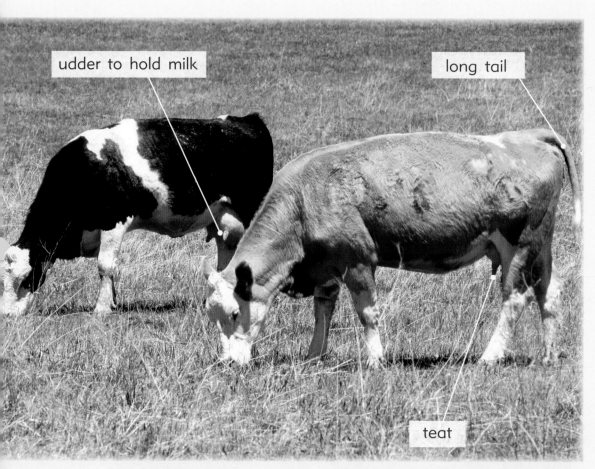

udder to hold milk

long tail

teat

A cow stores milk in her udder, ready for the calf to drink it.

Bulls

Bulls are bigger than cows. They are very heavy. Many bulls have horns, but some are **polled**.

stocky body

thick skin called hide

hooves

Not all bulls have horns.

Life Cycle

Calves grow up to have calves of their own, and the life cycle continues.

A calf can walk when it is only half an hour old.

A calf can do without its mother's milk when it is six months old. If it is female, it is now called a heifer. If it is male, it is now called a bull calf.

An adult bull and cow **mate** to produce a calf. A cow can have one calf every year.

Calves

New calves drink from their mother until they are six months old. If the mother dies, the farmer must feed the calves from a bottle.

The cow's milk makes the calf strong and protects it from disease.

Farm Life

On farms, bulls are often kept in a different field from the cows. Some fields have **barbed wire** or electric fences to keep in the strong bulls.

The bull gets a small shock if it tries to get through the electric fence.

Cattle stay together in a herd. They spend the day eating and resting. They **groom** themselves, or each other, by licking.

Cattle lick their coats and rub off insects.

Eating

Cattle eat grass. They pull the grass into their mouths with their tongues, because they have no top front teeth. In a week, a cow can eat its own weight in grass.

Cattle spend about six hours a day eating.

Farmers give cattle extra feed such as hay. They sometimes mix grain such as corn or barley in with the hay.

hay

barley

corn

Chewing the Cud

Cattle chew the **cud** for about eight hours a day. Once they have chewed and swallowed their food, they bring it back up from their stomach to chew again.

After eating, cattle sit down to chew the cud.

Cattle have four sections in their stomachs.

How cattle eat

- Half-chewed grass passes into the rumen.
- It then moves to the reticulum and is softened into cuds.
- The cuds go back to the mouth for more chewing. The chewed cuds are then stored in the rumen.
- Next, they pass into the omasum to be broken up.
- Finally, the broken-up cuds pass to the abomasum.

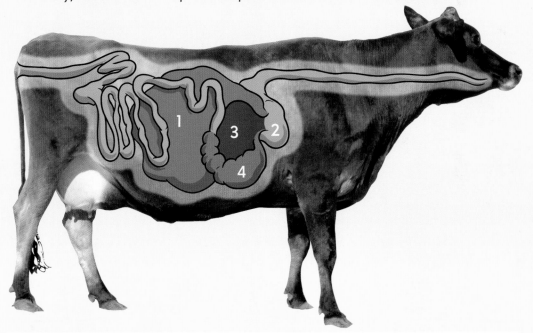

Key

1 rumen (roo-men)

2 reticulum (re-tick-you-lum)

3 omasum (oh-may-sum)

4 abomasum (ab-oh-may-sum)

Playing

Calves play with other calves. Sometimes they buck, kicking out with their back legs. They are also very curious. They run around the field and explore every corner.

Calves explore the fields together.

Sleeping

To sleep, cattle find a sheltered spot where they can turn their backs to the wind. Then they sit down and rest.

Cattle use trees for shelter when they sleep.

Cattle Farming

Some farms keep cows for their milk. These farms are called dairy farms. Later, the milk is made into butter, ice cream, yogurt, or cheese at a factory.

Products made with cows' milk are called dairy products.

ice cream

cheese

Other farms keep cattle for their meat. The meat is called beef. Cattle skins are made into leather for shoes, clothes, and furniture.

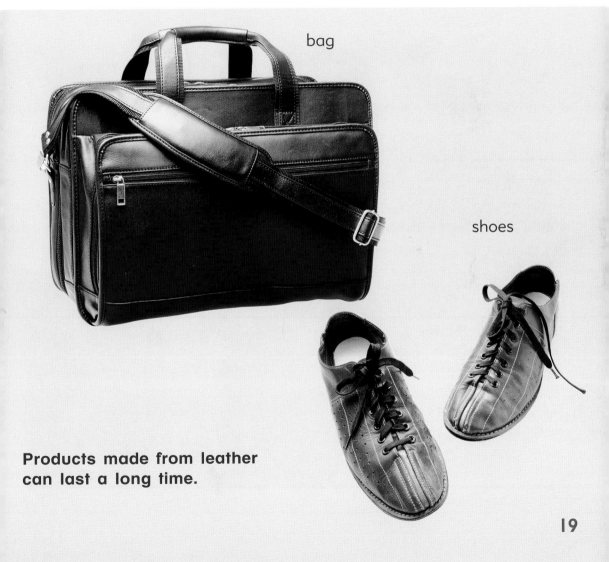

bag

shoes

Products made from leather can last a long time.

Cattle Breeds

Farmers keep different **breeds** of cattle for different purposes. Dairy cows are kept for their milk. They have long legs and bony bodies.

Jersey cattle are a light honey color with white spots. Their milk is very rich and creamy. It is good for making butter.

Holstein Friesian cattle are white with big black spots. One cow can produce up to 2,600 gallons of milk per year.

Beef cattle are kept for their meat. They usually have wider, fleshier bodies. They often have a thick neck and short legs.

Hereford cattle are red and white. Some have horns and others are polled. They produce a lot of meat.

Angus cattle grow to adult size very quickly. They produce high-quality meat that sells for a high price.

Looking After Cattle

Farmers need to keep track of all their cattle so they can look after them. To do this, farmers usually **brand** the cattle. This leaves a mark to show who owns them.

Cattle on large cattle farms are often branded.

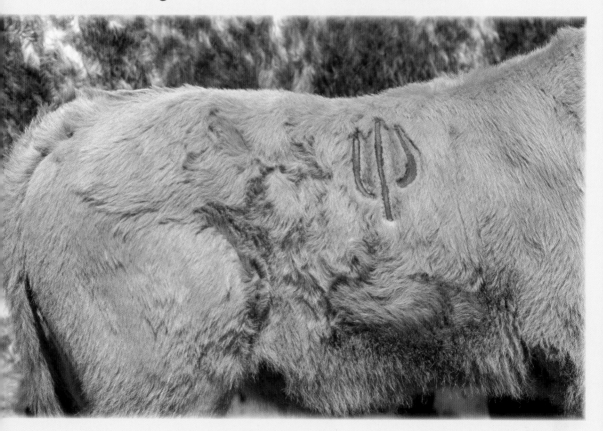

Some cattle have an ear tag that has a number on it. Farmers keep a record of all the numbers. This allows farmers to record information about each animal.

Ear tags are put in when the calves are very young.

Sheltering

In very cold places, dairy cows are housed in a shed or barn to keep them warm. Farmers put fresh straw in the barn every day.

Straw can be stored in the barn and fed to the cattle daily.

In some places, beef cattle farms are very big. These are called cattle ranches. The herd can be spread over many miles and the cattle can use trees for shelter.

Farmers sometimes need helicopters to help round up the cattle.

Feeding

When cattle eat the grass short in one **pasture**, the farmer moves them to a new one. If there is not enough grass, the farmer gives the cattle extra feed.

Hay is thrown from the back of a trailer or motorbike.

Watering

All cattle need water. Farmers must make sure there is enough fresh water, every day. Dairy cows need a lot of water to make milk.

Cattle drink from water troughs.

Milking

Dairy cows must be milked twice a day. A full udder is very heavy for the cow. Cows are often waiting at the milking shed when the farmer arrives.

Most farmers have a machine to milk a number of cows at one time.

How to Milk a Cow

You will need
- milk bucket
- stool

What to do

1 Put the milk bucket under the teat to be milked. Sit on the stool, near the udder.

2 With your thumb and pointing finger, pinch the teat and push up close to the udder. Pull down and as you do, squeeze the teat with your other fingers.

3 Let go. Then repeat step 2.

Farmers can milk cows with two hands.

Farm Facts

- A cow must drink two pints of fresh, clean water for every one pint of milk she makes.

- Cows have an amazing sense of smell. They can detect scents more than six miles away.

- Cattle can see in color, except for red.

- Cows chew about 41,630 times a day.

- The average cow produces about 90 glasses of milk a day.

Glossary

barbed wire   steel wire with sharp, twisted spikes used in fences

brand   a mark made on the skin of an animal, often by burning, to show ownership

breed   a group of animals that have the same set of features

cud   small wad of half-chewed grass inside a cow's stomach

groom   to clean an animal's fur

mate   when a male and female join to create their young

pasture   a field of grass

polled   bred without horns

udder   a cow's milk bag

Index